KATIE MORAG
AND THE BIG BOY COUSINS

High Farm

The Holiday House

Mrs Bayview's

The Lady Arti

e Redburn Bridge

The Village

THE ISLE of STRUAY

Grannie's

The Mainland

The Jetty

ISLE of STRUAY
SHOP & POST OFFICE

OBAN
TIMES
GET
YOUR COPY
HERE

The Shop & Post Office

To all who cope with temptation

First published in Great Britain by The Bodley Head Ltd in 1987
First published in Picture Lions in 1990
This edition published in 1992
10 9 8 7 6 5 4 3 2
Picture Lions is an imprint of the Children's Division,
part of HarperCollins Publishers Limited,
77-85 Fulham Palace Road, Hammersmith,
London W6 8JB

Printed and bound in Hong Kong

KATIE MORAG AND THE BIG BOY COUSINS

Mairi Hedderwick

PictureLions

An Imprint of HarperCollinsPublishers

It was the second fortnight in July, and Katie Morag's Big Boy Cousins had arrived from the Mainland to camp at Grannie Island's, as they did each summer.

"Oh, no!" sighed the islanders. "Here they come AGAIN!"
The Big Boy Cousins were very wild and unruly. Katie Morag thought they were wonderful.

"Why do you put up with them, Grannie Island?" cried the McColls. "Nobody else will have them!" declared Grannie Island. "And I need some help with the chores." Grannie Island loaded the provisions

into her tractor and trailer, ready for the journey back to her house. "Coming, Katie Morag?" smiled the biggest Boy Cousin, Hector.

Soon the tent was pitched and the stores unloaded.

"Now," called Grannie Island. "There are potatoes to be dug up, peats to be fetched and driftwood to be gathered. Who is doing what?"

"GEE WHILICKERS!" groaned Hector, Archie, Jamie, Dougal and Murdo Iain.

Everyone pretended not to hear Grannie Island, even Katie Morag. They hid down by the shore.

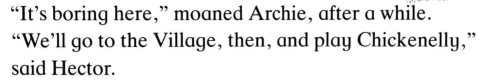

"It's boring here," moaned Archie, after a while.
"We'll go to the Village, then, and play Chickenelly,"
said Hector.
"Yeah!" chorused all the Big Boy Cousins –
except for Murdo Iain.
"It's an awful long walk," he whined.

"I know a quick way," chirped up Katie Morag.
She was enjoying being naughty and continued to ignore Grannie Island's cries for help.

ALICE

In the Village all was calm and peaceful. The villagers were inside their houses, having a well-earned rest after a morning's hard work.

Nobody noticed Grannie Island's heavily laden boat, heading across the Bay.

On the door:

BACK
LATER

SURGERY
HOURS

Chickenelly was a daring game.
"Last one gets caught!" whispered Hector, as he led all
the cousins on tiptoe round the gable end of Nurse's house.
Katie Morag's tummy tickled inside with excitement.

Then the Big Boy Cousins and Katie Morag ran quickly down the length of the village, banging very loudly on each back door.

BANG–a–BANG–a–BANG–a–BANG–a–BANG!

In their mad rush to get to the other end of the village they knocked into all sorts of things, and nobody saw Grannie Island racing round the head of the Bay on her tractor.

"And just WHAT do you think you are all up to?" Grannie Island was colossal with fury.

"Chickenelly," said Katie Morag, timidly, wishing she had never heard of the game.

"Gee whilickers!" groaned Hector, Archie, Jamie, Dougal and Murdo Iain.

Grannie Island made them all apologize to the upset villagers and told them to clear up the mess they had caused.

"And you can all WALK back when you are finished!" she shouted.

Even though Grannie Island was angry outside, Katie Morag knew her Grannie was sad inside, and that made Katie Morag feel sad, too.

Tired and very hungry, the Big Boy Cousins were silent on the long journey back to Grannie Island's.

Katie Morag walked as fast as she could.

"We've got to say sorry to Grannie," she said.
"*And* help her with the chores."
"Gee whilickers!" groaned Hector, Archie, Jamie, Dougal *and* Murdo Iain.

The chores didn't take that long once everyone lent a hand.
Katie Morag worked hardest of them all, and she made sure that the
Big Boy Cousins didn't skive.

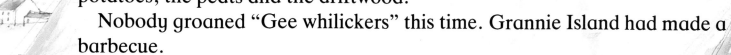

"Last chore!" called a smiling Grannie Island. "Bring over some of the potatoes, the peats and the driftwood."

Nobody groaned "Gee whilickers" this time. Grannie Island had made a barbecue.

"This is what I would call a hard-earned feast," said Grannie Island, dishing out mounds of fried tatties and beans.

"Tomorrow–" she continued – "*after* the chores, we'll go fishing and see what we can catch for another feast."

"*Not* chickenellies!" giggled Katie Morag.

And when it came to toasting the marshmallows, Katie Morag made sure Grannie Island got the biggest one.
That was fair, wasn't it?

Here are some more Picture Lions

for you to enjoy